POPULAR CULTURE

A VIEW FROM THE PAPARAZZI

Orlando Bloom	John Legend
Kelly Clarkson	Lindsay Lohan
Johnny Depp	Mandy Moore
Hilary Duff	Ashlee and Jessica Simpson
Will Ferrell	
Jake Gyllenhaal	Justin Timberlake
Paris and Nicky Hilton	Owen and Luke Wilson
LeBron James	Tiger Woods

Justin Timberlake

South Huntington Pub. Lib.
145 Pidgeon Hill Rd.
Huntington Sta., N.Y. 11746

Hal Marcovitz

Mason Crest Publishers

Justin Timberlake

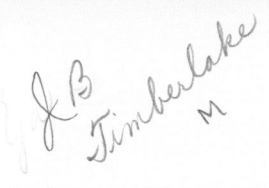

FRONTIS
American singer Justin Timberlake has won four Grammy Awards and sold over 13 million albums worldwide.

Produced by 21st Century Publishing and Communications, Inc.

Copyright © 2008 by Mason Crest Publishers. All rights reserved. No part of this publication may be reproduced or transmitted in any form or by any means, electronic or mechanical, including photocopying, recording, taping, or any information storage and retrieval system, without permission from the publisher.

MASON CREST PUBLISHERS INC.
370 Reed Road
Broomall, Pennsylvania 19008
(866) MCP-BOOK (toll free)
www.masoncrest.com

Printed in the United States.

First Printing

9 8 7 6 5 4 3 2 1

Library of Congress Cataloging-in-Publication Data

Marcovitz, Hal.
　Justin Timberlake / Hal Marcovitz.
　　p. cm.— 　(Pop culture : a view from the paparazzi)
　Includes bibliographical references (p.　), discography (p.　), filmography (p.　), and index.
　Hardback edition: ISBN-13: 978-1-4222-0209-8
　Paperback edition: ISBN-13: 978-1-4222-0364-4
　1. Timberlake, Justin, 1981–　—Juvenile literature. 2. 'N Sync (Musical group)—Juvenile literature. 3. Singers—United States—Biography—Juvenile literature. I. Title.
ML3930.T58M37 2008
782.42164092—dc22
[B]　　　　　　　　　　　　　　　　　　　　　　　　　　　　　　　2007018486

Publisher's notes:
- All quotations in this book come from original sources, and contain the spelling and grammatical inconsistencies of the original text.

- The Web sites mentioned in this book were active at the time of publication. The publisher is not responsible for Web sites that have changed their addresses or discontinued operation since the date of publication. The publisher will review and update the Web site addresses each time the book is reprinted.

CONTENTS

1	**Vindicated**	7
2	**Born Ready**	13
3	**Breaking Away**	25
4	**Flying Solo**	33
5	**Limitless Options**	45
	Chronology	56
	Accomplishments & Awards	57
	Further Reading & Internet Resources	60
	Glossary	61
	Index	62
	Picture Credits	64
	About the Author	64

Justin Timberlake poses with the two Grammy Awards that he received at the 46th annual awards ceremony held in Los Angeles, February 8, 2004. His hit song "Cry Me a River" won the award for Best Male Pop Vocal Performance, and his bestselling solo album *Justified* was named Best Pop Vocal Album.

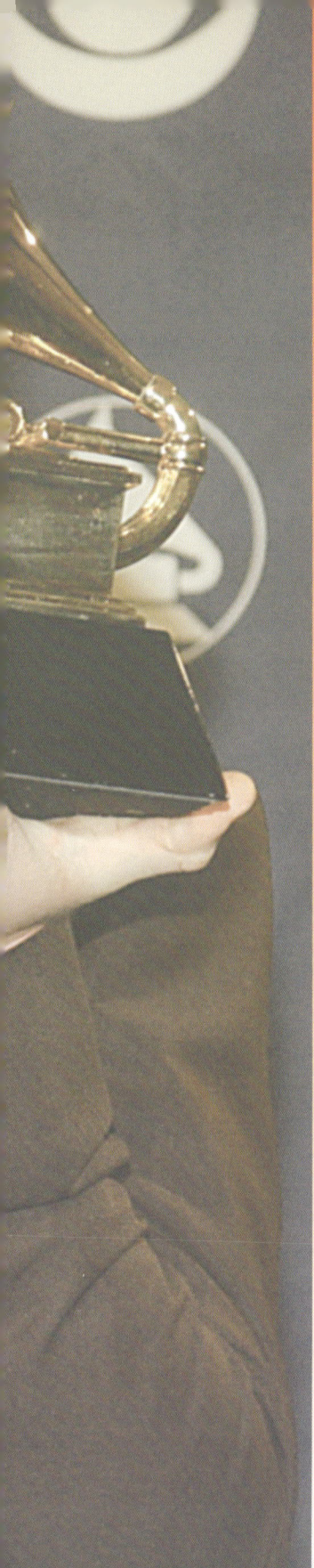

1

Vindicated

People who tuned into the Grammy Awards telecast on the night of February 8, 2004, found plenty of glamour, excitement, good music and, above all else, high drama. That's because just a week before the telecast, two of the music industry's biggest stars, Justin Timberlake and Janet Jackson, had been involved in a controversial halftime show during the Super Bowl.

At the Super Bowl, one of the world's premiere sporting events, Justin and Janet sang the song "Rock Your Body" before 71,000 fans in Houston's Reliant Stadium, as well as a worldwide television audience of some 90 million viewers. As the song neared its conclusion, Justin reached over and pulled down Jackson's black leather top, exposing the singer's breast. The impromptu striptease was unintentional—Justin's motion was supposed to have revealed a red garment underneath, but it came off unexpectedly. Although the incident lasted for no more than a few seconds, it stirred a national furor with the blame falling mostly on the two stars. Few people seemed to accept Justin's exasperated contention that the breast-baring episode was due to a "wardrobe malfunction."

A week later, Justin arrived at the Staples Center in Los Angeles, California, for what he hoped would be a moment of triumph. More than a year before, Justin had released his first solo album, *Justified*. The CD quickly caught fire, eventually selling more than 7 million copies, and Justin had been nominated for five Grammy Awards.

Major Step Forward

Justified represented a major step forward in Justin's career. Before the album was released, the 21-year-old singer had been primarily known as one of the young singers in the enormously popular all-boy group 'N Sync. The group specialized in pop and dance music, appealing mostly to young girls. With *Justified*, Justin hoped to show a wider range that included rhythm and blues (R&B) as well as steamy love songs. The album featured such hit singles as "Like I Love You" and "Cry Me a River." Barry Weiss, the president of Justin's record company, Jive Records, told *Billboard* magazine,

> "This is a groundbreaking record that perfectly merges great artistry and commercial viability. The fact that people are so receptive to 'Like I Love You' indicates that they're ready to embrace Justin in a new light. We believe that people will be blown away when they experience the rest of the album."

The album itself stirred a bit of controversy. Just before going into the **studio** to cut the record, Justin broke up with his girlfriend, pop star Britney Spears. The two singers had known each other since they had starred together on *The All-New Mickey Mouse Club*, a Disney Channel variety show for young viewers. Eventually, Justin and Britney rose to stardom and started dating. But after a three-year relationship, Britney broke it off. The **tabloid** press reported that she had started dating other celebrities, particularly Swedish model Marcus Schenkenberg.

Vindicated

Janet Jackson and Justin perform a medley of their hits "Rhythm Nation" and "Rock Your Body" during the Super Bowl XXXVIII halftime show in February 2004. At the end of the song, Justin reached over and tore off part of Janet's costume, revealing her breast to the television audience of more than 90 million people.

Feeling Betrayed

Justin felt betrayed, and used the video for "Cry Me a River" to make his feelings known. The song tells the story of a lover spurned. In the video, Justin breaks into his old girlfriend's home, where he finds a video camera and films himself kissing his new girlfriend. Before

JUSTIN TIMBERLAKE

leaving the home, Justin plays the video on the home's TV, where it is discovered by his old girlfriend—who looks remarkably like Britney Spears, down to her blond tresses, newsboy cap, and tattoo on her lower back.

Music critics thought the video contained too many cruel stabs at Spears. Said *Rolling Stone* writer Erik Hedegaard:

Two workers place a large poster promoting Justin's solo album *Justified* outside of a Hollywood record store. The award-winning album showed that Justin was a talented singer who was willing to experiment with a more mature sound. *Justified* launched a brilliant solo career for the young singer, eventually selling more than 7 million copies worldwide.

> **"If the Britney figure is a cheater, the Justin character is both a cheater and a creep.... It's weird, all right, and speaks of a guy with a mother-size hole in his heart who wants to get even and then some."**

As for Justin, he shrugged off the criticism. "What can I say?" he responded, when Hedegaard asked him about the video's content. "I don't want anyone to come off smelling like roses. I don't like the smell of roses, anyway."

The video for "Cry Me a River" helped spark sales, and Justin worked very hard to sell the album. He went on a long concert tour with pop singer Christina Aguilera. In each city, after playing the large **venues** with Aguilera, Justin took his band into small nightclubs where he performed shows for small audiences anxious to see him sing without all the **pyrotechnics** surrounding the big stage productions. He also made a number of network TV appearances, including a gig as the guest host of *Saturday Night Live*, which showed he had a flair for acting and comedy. He gave numerous interviews to magazine and newspaper reporters.

Brilliant Career

As Grammy night approached, Justin learned that CBS network executives were concerned about the audience reaction to his appearance on the show. They demanded that if he took the stage in the Staples Center, he would have to issue an apology for the Super Bowl incident. Justin agreed. Approaching the microphone, he said:

> **"I know it's been a rough week on everybody, and, um, what occurred was unintentional, completely regrettable, and I apologize if you guys were offended."**

For Justin, the night turned out to be more than just an opportunity to apologize. Justin won two Grammy Awards, proving his talent. The awards also provided a measure of vindication, showing that the incident at the Super Bowl had been nothing more than an embarrassing moment in what was otherwise turning into a brilliant music career.

Lynn Harless poses with her son Justin at a Beverly Hills party, 2007. Lynn was one of the first people who believed that Justin could be a talented singer. After hearing him perform at a school talent show, she hired a local voice teacher, Bob Westbrook, to give Justin singing lessons.

2

Born Ready

When Justin Timberlake was eight years old, he got together with four friends to enter a talent show at his elementary school in Millington, Tennessee, a town near Memphis. Justin and his friends decided to **lip synch** a song recorded by one of the biggest acts in music at the time—the all-boy singing group New Kids on the Block.

The act turned out to be a big hit—all the girls in the audience shrieked and screamed as though they were watching the actual band perform on stage. The girls made so much noise that few people in the audience could tell that one of the boys, Justin, wasn't lip synching—he was actually singing. One person who heard Justin's voice was his mother, Lynn Harless. Until then, Justin had displayed little interest in performing in front of an audience. Listening to her son on stage, Harless believed he had talent.

Harless videotaped the talent show. She took the tape to a local voice teacher, Bob Westbrook, and played the tape. According to author Sean Smith, she asked Westbrook, "Don't you think we ought to start giving him some lessons?" The teacher agreed, and Justin soon became one of Westbrook's students.

Musical Family

Memphis, Tennessee, has a rich musical heritage. The nightclubs along the city's Beale Street have spawned some of the country's top rhythm and blues performers, such as Howlin' Wolf, Ike Turner, and B.B. King. R&B has its roots in folk music performed by African-American musicians, who updated the sounds to include strong beats that reflect the influences of urban living. Memphis is located in the heart of the South, which means country music dominates the local airwaves. The city was the home of Elvis Presley, the enormously popular entertainer who until his death in 1977 lived in an ornate mansion there known as Graceland. Presley managed to straddle several genres: in addition to his many rock 'n' roll hits, he also recorded country hits and knew how to sing soulful blues songs.

Music is important in the lives of a lot of people in the Memphis area, and the Timberlakes were no exception. Justin's grandfather, Bill Bomar, was an accomplished guitarist. Justin's father, Randall Timberlake, directed the choir at a local church. Later, Justin told *Rolling Stone*:

> "I grew up listening to country music. I listened to things that were out on the radio, but also my grandfather taught me about Johnny Cash and Willie Nelson and the importance that they had and how they were ambassadors of country music."

Justin Randall Timberlake was born January 31, 1981. He seemed to have a natural musical ability—as a baby, his mother recalled watching him kick his feet in time to music. But Justin would not receive formal training in music at home. His parents were divorced when he was five. Soon, his mother married Paul Harless, a Millington banker.

Born Ready

Justin grew up listening to the music of Elvis Presley, and has even been compared to Elvis and other early rock 'n' roll stars. "He's got It, whatever It is," producer Jimmy Jam told *People* magazine in 2003. "Whatever the Elvises had back in their day. What It is for this generation, Justin has got it."

JUSTIN TIMBERLAKE

The Harless home in Shelby Forest, a Millington neighborhood, was warm and loving and Paul accepted Justin as a son. For Justin, it was a typical, middle-class upbringing. He was a quiet child who did well at E.E. Jeter Elementary School, loved to play basketball and video games, and owned a mutt named Scooter.

Showing Off His Talent

But then came the Jeter talent show, followed by the lessons from Westbrook. Within a few months of starting voice lessons, Justin emerged as Westbrook's top student. Soon, he started entering, and winning, talent contests throughout Tennessee. In 1992, at the age of 11, he won a talent contest known as the Universal Charm Pageant across the state in Nashville. In the contest, he sang the soulful ballad, "When a Man Loves a Woman." The blond, curly-haired boy impressed the judges not only with his singing talent, but also with his dancing ability and stage presence. When Justin stepped in front of the audience, he seemed to light up the stage. The prize was $16,000—the largest award he had ever earned in a talent show. In addition, the win brought him his first press attention. A reporter for the *Memphis Commercial-Appeal* covered the competition and wrote:

> "His baby-blue eyes beam. His mound of golden blond hair sweeps back. His wide, pearly smile flashes. His trained soprano voice rolls, trills, yodels and twangs.... Justin Randall Timberlake, eleven, may be just another kid in the legions who dream about becoming a singing star. But this sixth grader from Shelby Forest who sings country and pop has bolted out of the chute toward his dream."

Soon after the Universal Charm Pageant, Lynn Harless learned that a national TV show, *Star Search*, was holding **auditions** for new contestants. Under the show's rules, contestants who were picked to perform competed against one another in several competitions, including singing, dancing and acting. Justin agreed to enter, and along with his mother traveled to Orlando, Florida, for the audition.

He came up short, beaten out for a place on the show by another contestant. But while staying in Orlando, Harless learned that another national show, *The All-New Mickey Mouse Club*, was also screening talent. Justin auditioned for the producers and was picked.

Born Ready

When he competed in talent shows as a grade-school student, Justin impressed the judges with his good looks and stage presence as well as his singing ability. He won several important talent contests in Tennessee before starting to enter national contests looking for talented young people like the television show *Star Search*.

Becoming a Mouseketeer

The All-New Mickey Mouse Club was an updated version of a very popular children's variety program made by the Disney studio that had aired during the 1950s. Several child performers from the original show went on to careers in entertainment, most notably movie star Annette Funicello. In the new version, which was entering its sixth season, the producers wanted to appeal to a young and hip audience. They looked for performers who had energy and talent to take on the roles of the 20 "Mousekeeters." In addition to Justin, they selected two other performers who had failed their *Star Search* auditions, Britney Spears and Christina Aguilera.

For Justin and his mother, the show represented a major change in their lives. They would have to live in Orlando for six months out of the year. Justin had to drop out of school; he would be taught by **tutors** hired by Disney. The hours promised to be long—three hours of tutoring in the morning, followed by several hours of rehearsals and taping.

Justin and the other Mouseketeers rose to the challenge. They brought a zeal and electricity to the show, singing, dancing, acting and performing in **sketch comedy** routines. What's more, the producers hoped to address some serious topics faced by young people, such as eating disorders, racism, and depression. At times Justin and the others found themselves playing dramatic roles.

The hours may have been long and the work hard but for the young entertainers, the education they received from the Disney voice coaches, **choreographers**, and acting teachers was priceless. During his two years as a Mouseketeer, Justin polished his dancing, found more range in his voice, and learned how to connect with audiences. He later told author K.M. Squires:

> "It was a great experience all around. The whole thing was amazing for me."

The Birth of 'N Sync

Most television shows do not run for very long. In February 1995, Disney canceled the *All-New Mickey Mouse Club.* Justin returned to school in Millington, but his life as an ordinary teenager didn't last long. That summer, he received a call from Chris Kirkpatrick, whom he had known casually in Orlando. Kirkpatrick was a professional singer who performed for visitors at Walt Disney World.

Born Ready 19

Some of the cast members of *The All-New Mickey Mouse Club* pose for a photograph. In addition to Justin (back row, third from left), several other performers on the Disney Channel show eventually became incredibly successful pop stars, including Christina Aguilera (front left) and Britney Spears (center). Justin appeared on the show during its last two seasons on the air.

JUSTIN TIMBERLAKE

After *The All-New Mickey Mouse Club* was canceled in 1995, another former Disney employee invited Justin to join an all-male singing group. Justin jumped at the chance to join the band, which would become 'N Sync. In addition to Justin (front, seated), the group included (clockwise from left) J.C. Chasez, Chris Kirpatrick, Joey Fatone, and Lance Bass.

    Kirkpatrick had been a finalist for the Backstreet Boys, a very successful all-male singing group. Although he wasn't selected, the band's manager, Lou Pearlman, told Kirkpatrick that he planned to organize a second group and wanted Kirkpatrick to be a part of it. He asked Kirkpatrick to recruit additional singers for the new group.

    Kirkpatrick called Justin at his home in Millington, because he knew about his success on the *All New Mickey Mouse Club* and thought he would fit in with the new group. He asked if Justin would go to Florida and audition for the group. Justin didn't hesitate. Within hours, he and his mother were on a plane back to Orlando.

The other members of the group quickly fell into place. In addition to Kirkpatrick and Justin, the others who joined were J.C. Chasez, a former Mouseketeer who had taken a job as a waiter after the show folded; Joey Fatone, a kid from New York City who, like Kirkpatrick, was working as a singer at a theme park, and Lance Bass, who had been recommended by Bob Westbrook.

The group spent months in rehearsal while Pearlman planned a European tour for his new boy band. At this point, the band had no name. Shortly after a rehearsal, Lynn and Paul Harless joined the boys for a meal at an Orlando restaurant. As the boys kicked around ideas for a name, author Sean Smith reported, Lynn Harless made a suggestion. "You know," she said, "these guys just sound so tight together, they sound very much in sync." Everyone agreed, and decided to name the band 'N Sync.

Becoming Stars

Early in 1996 the new members of 'N Sync left the United States for Stockholm, Sweden, where they would record songs for their first album. At the time the Backstreet Boys were emerging as major recording stars, particularly in Europe, where they had legions of fans. Pearlman hoped that his new band could absorb some of the popularity of the earlier group, so he matched up 'N Sync with Swedish songwriters Dag Volle and Max Martin, who had written some of the Backstreet Boys' biggest hits. In October 1996, Pearlman released 'N Sync's first single, "I Want You Back," to radio stations in Germany. It proved to be an immediate success, getting plenty of air play on radio shows and climbing to the top of the German music charts within a week of its release.

The boys made a video for "I Want You Back," toured Germany, and received their first dose of what it was like to be stars. At every stop on the tour, they were greeted by hordes of young girls who shrieked and rushed them as they got off their tour bus; sometimes, the boys had to fight their way onto the stage. The tour also turned out to be a grind. Between October 7, the day the single was released, and November 9, they performed more than 30 shows. But their efforts paid off. By December 16, the group's debut album, titled *'N Sync*, had sold more

JUSTIN TIMBERLAKE

'N Sync gained valuable experience by performing in Europe, where they recorded and released their first album in 1996. By the end of the next year, they had played shows for screaming crowds in many countries. Once they had established a strong international fan base, their debut album was released in the United States.

than 250,000 copies in Germany. Fans in other countries had taken notice as well, and were anxious to buy the album, so Pearlman expanded the tour to include Great Britain, Sweden, Poland, Mexico, and South Africa.

By the end of 1997 'N Sync had proven to be a major success in Europe and elsewhere. However, nobody in the United States had heard of them yet. That would soon change. On March 24, 1998, Pearlman released *'N Sync* in the United States. The album got off to a healthy start, debuting in ninth place on the pop music charts compiled by *Billboard* magazine. That July, the band got a huge dose of national exposure when the Backstreet Boys backed out of a nationally televised concert promoted by the Disney studio. With Disney desperate to find a substitute, Pearlman suggested 'N Sync. The concert was taped at Walt Disney World in Orlando—a fitting venue, given the fact that two of the band members were former Mouseketeers.

Justin and the others put on a terrific performance, helping to boost sales and keep their debut album on the *Billboard* pop charts for months. All of the band members were excited at their success. Fatone told *People* magazine:

> **"We knew we were going to be successful, but we didn't know it was going to happen as fast as it did or as big."**

The members of 'N Sync pose with a surfboard at the 1999 Teen Choice Awards. From the time the group emerged on the U.S. music scene, 'N Sync proved to be exceptionally popular, particularly among young girls. The band won a dozen Teen Choice Awards and sold millions of albums.

3
Breaking Away

As 'N Sync performed on national TV during the Walt Disney World concert in 1998, viewers at home could not help but notice that two of the young singers seemed to stand out from the others. Justin Timberlake and J.C. Chasez, the two former Mouseketeers, knew how to play to the camera and hold the audience's attention.

One of the viewers at home was Chuck Yerger, the Disney tutor who taught the two boys during their Mouseketeer days and knew them well. He told author Sean Smith:

JUSTIN TIMBERLAKE

> "They had watched themselves so often on tape that they instinctively knew what was a good move for the camera. As you watched the group progress, it was obvious Justin and J.C. were the centerpieces."

In fact, as 'N Sync became more of a presence in the entertainment world, Justin emerged as the performer who seemed to be capturing more attention than the others. Many 'N Sync fans thought he was the best singer and best dancer, and were captivated by his electric smile. Bob Fischetti, an assistant to Lou Pearlman, told Smith,

> "The biggest thing that ever stays in my mind with that kid is his million-dollar smile. It could be mischievous; it could be innocent or smirky, or whatever kids wanted, but it always had a kind of cocky confidence, reflecting who he was, not in a bad way, but in a 100 percent great way. It gave him an aura."

For his part, Justin had no intention of upstaging his fellow band mates. He had a lot of respect for their talents. "We're not just a recording group, we're friends," Justin told *Billboard*. "We're growing and changing and making music that is real and honest. . . . As long as we continue to remain true to who we are, we have a fair shot at being heard. That's all we've ever really wanted: to be heard."

Hectic Schedule

Following the U.S. release of their debut album, band members found themselves riding a roller coaster to the top of the entertainment world. Their schedule was overwhelming. In the year following the album's release, Pearlman booked them for a nationwide tour that spanned 100 concert dates—including some in which they opened for Janet Jackson during her tour to promote her album, *Velvet Rope*. For months, the band seemed everywhere. Jay Leno invited them to appear on *The Tonight Show*. Government officials in the Caribbean islands of St. Vincent and the Grenadines put their images on postage stamps. The Kellogg cereal company put their pictures on boxes of Corn Pops cereal. The busy schedule helped the band sell more than 7 million copies of *'N Sync*.

During that hectic year, the band members had just enough time to stop in Orlando and record their second album—a CD of Christmas

Breaking Away

"The best part of this is doing what we like to do with our friends," Justin told *People* magazine in 1999, commenting on 'N Sync's popularity. Many fans of the group felt that Justin stood out from the other members. However, he always tried to downplay such suggestions, noting that all five band members had contributed to 'N Sync's success.

songs titled *Home for Christmas*. Justin performed a solo on the album, singing the Christmas carol "O Holy Night." The album was thrown together quickly to take advantage of the Christmas shopping season in late 1998. Nevertheless, owing to 'N Sync's enormous popularity, *Home for Christmas* sold more than 4 million copies.

'N Sync's schedule was so hectic that Justin found it hard to maintain a personal life. In 1998, he had been reunited with his former friend from the Mouseketeers, Britney Spears. When she joined the *All-New Mickey Mouse Club* in 1993, Britney was 11 years old. Now, at the age of 17, she had grown into a sexy, sizzling entertainer. She joined 'N Sync on tour as the band's opening act. Soon, Justin and Britney found themselves in a romantic relationship.

Justin had dated before, but Britney was his first serious girlfriend. He believed he could spend the rest of his life with her. But as Justin's feelings for Britney intensified, the two stars found it difficult to spend more than a few days at a time together. Justin had to maintain a busy schedule performing with 'N Sync; meanwhile, Britney had scored a major hit with the single "Baby One More Time," and soon started her own tour. Their time away from one another would eventually lead to a bitter breakup that Justin blamed on her unfaithfulness to him. He told *Rolling Stone*:

> **"She has a beautiful heart, but if I've lost my trust in someone, I don't think it's right for me to be with them."**

Legal Troubles

Justin was encountering problems professionally as well. Soon after *Home for Christmas* was released, the band members approached Pearlman and demanded that he renegotiate their contract. Although they were being well-paid—Justin used his earnings to buy an expensive Mercedes Benz sports car—the boys felt that Pearlman was raking in millions of dollars and that their share of the profits should be much larger. The 1999 tour earned $44 million just from ticket sales. Sales of albums and band merchandise brought in tens of millions more.

Pearlman refused to renegotiate. The boys responded by refusing to record for RCA Records again. Pearlman then slapped the band members with a **lawsuit**, demanding $150 million and preventing them from recording for any other label or using the name 'N Sync.

Breaking Away

Britney Spears and Justin pose for a photograph, 1999. The two had met on the *All-New Mickey Mouse Club* back in 1993, but did not start dating until 1998. By that time Britney was becoming pop music's hottest artist, winning awards for her albums *Baby One More Time* and *Oops!... I Did it Again*.

The boys responded with their own lawsuit, demanding $25 million from Pearlman. For the young band members, it was a tense and frightening time as they came to grips with the possibility that the extensive legal wrangling could cost them their careers. Justin told *Face* magazine:

JUSTIN TIMBERLAKE

> "It was horrible and the biggest low point. It's the one time I honestly said, 'I don't want to do this anymore.' I thought our careers were over."

In December 1999, the boys faced Pearlman in court. Under orders from the judge, the attorneys met privately and worked out a settlement. While most of the details of the settlement have never been

In court papers filed as part of their lawsuit seeking to get out of their contract with Lou Pearlman, the members of 'N Sync called their former manager "a con man . . . who has become wealthy at ['N Sync's] expense. They have been cheated at every turn by Pearlman's fraud, manipulation, and breach of fiduciary duty."

revealed, it was clear that both sides won something. Pearlman would continue to share in the profits from 'N Sync's records, but the band was now free to make its own deals with a new record label. 'N Sync soon signed with Jive Records, which produced albums for Spears and the Backstreet Boys.

No Strings Attached

With a new record deal in hand, the band members got down to producing what would be their most successful album. Released in March 2000, *No Strings Attached* would go on to sell 15 million copies. The top single from the album, "Bye Bye Bye," hit the top of the *Billboard* charts as soon as the album hit the stores.

Justin worked hard on *No Strings Attached*. He wrote one of the songs, "I'll be Good for You," and also spent hours in the studio helping the engineers tweak the sounds and beats. The album cover features the boys playing the roles of **marionettes**—it was clearly a statement about how they had been able to break away from Pearlman's control.

Justin said the album showed how the band members were growing up and exerting their independence. He said:

> "We have a very broad sound. There are different directions we can take it, so we did as much of that as we could on this album. That's why we called the album *No Strings Attached*. We have no strings to hold us down. We're ready to show the world that."

"I think this album is gonna be even more diverse— a little edgier into the R&B and dance," Justin told *Teen* magazine just before the release of *No Strings Attached*. "It's going to [be] a little more mature, but we're still gonna keep the harmonies because that's really our sound." *No Strings Attached* eventually sold over 15 million copies worldwide.

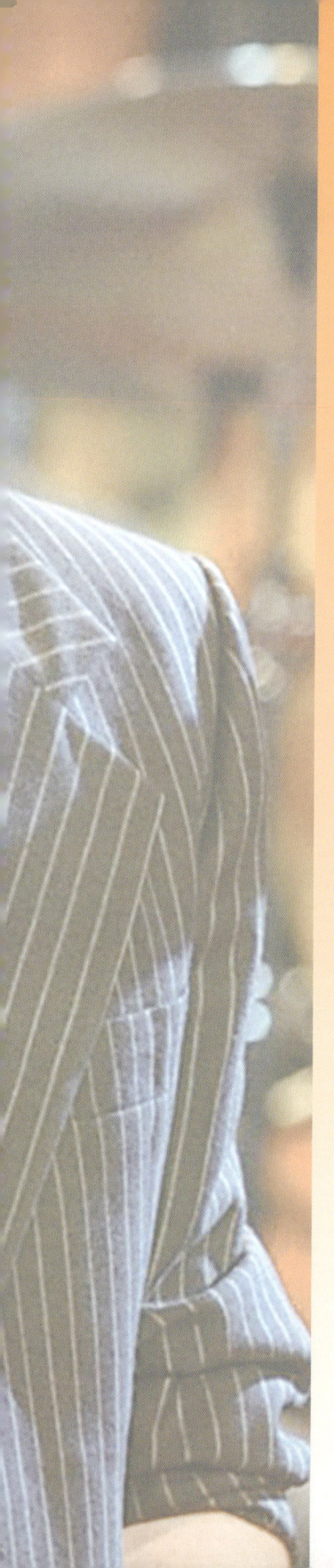

4

Flying Solo

As *No Strings Attached* climbed the charts and became a major success for Jive Records, readers of *People* magazine voted Justin Timberlake "The Most Beautiful Person in the World." Millions of people were clearly smitten by the young singer's chiseled good looks, talent, athletic dancing ability, and electric stage presence.

By now, 19-year-old Justin had grown into an American sex symbol. He kept fit by playing basketball—a sport he had loved since elementary school. As a young boy, Justin kept a poster of Chicago Bulls all-star Michael Jordon tacked to his wall. He also took up golf, a sport he grew to love because he could enjoy the company of his friends on a remote golf course without having to worry about screaming fans tearing at his clothes or asking for autographs. "I love golf because of my situation with work, all over the place all of the time," he told Sean Smith. "Playing golf, you're in one place for four-and-a-half or five hours. I can be by myself."

Still, as the *People* magazine poll showed, Justin's fans were not likely to be leaving him alone for long. It was becoming clear that among 'N Sync's five singers, Justin was the member with the most star potential.

Celebrity

'N Sync had recorded *No Strings Attached* as a statement: now independent of Lou Pearlman, they aimed to prove they could produce a hit album on their own. Musically, *No Strings Attached* wasn't that much different from their earlier work or from the albums produced by the other major boy groups of the era, such as the Backstreet Boys and New Kids on the Block. Most of the songs were gushy boy-falls-for-girl ballads, which given the robust sales of the album was evidently all right with 'N Sync's fans.

With their next album, *Celebrity*, Justin and the other band members hoped to take their music in a new direction. Growing up in the Memphis area, Justin had been exposed to R&B music at an early age. He convinced the rest of the group to introduce a measure of rhythm and blues into the songs on *Celebrity*. Veteran R&B producers Brian Traneau and the team of Pharrell Williams and Chad Hugo, who are known as the Neptunes, were hired to help fashion the songs in the studio.

Justin did more than perform on the album; he helped produce five of the tracks and co-wrote seven of the songs, including the single "Pop." In the song, Justin makes a statement that the riches and glitz of the music industry often cause artists to lose track of what's important—the music.

Celebrity was released in April 2001, and turned out to be a big success. The album eventually sold more than 5 million copies.

Back on Tour

As they had with *No Strings Attached*, 'N Sync went on a nationwide tour to promote *Celebrity*. The tour was an enormous undertaking, as the band was booked into the country's largest sports stadiums. It took more than 50 trucks and 24 buses to haul the sound and stage equipment, as well as the cast and crew, from city to city.

The show itself featured plenty of sound and light effects, computer-animated video projections, fireworks, and other pyrotechnics. To begin

Flying Solo

Justin warms up at the AT&T Pebble Beach National Pro-Am, an annual golf tournament that draws both celebrities and professional golfers. Justin took up golf in 2000 and soon became a very good player. His 10 handicap means that his average game is just 10 strokes over par—a very good score for an amateur golfer.

The members of 'N Sync drop onto stage on wires to open one of the concerts promoting their 2001 album *Celebrity*. **The album was another huge hit for 'N Sync, selling 5 million copies in the United States and 10 million worldwide. Three singles—"Pop," "Gone," and "Girlfriend"—were top-10 hits on Billboard's music charts.**

the concert, the boys dropped onto the stage on wires. They disappeared through trap doors, then appeared again elsewhere on stage. They rode mechanical bulls and were whisked across stage on a huge conveyor belt. In a *Boston Herald* article, music critic Sarah Rodman praised the tour's visit to Foxboro Stadium in Massachusetts, writing:

> "They've learned how to do behemoth absolutely right. In fact, the steadily maturing vocal quintet could give some of their elders a few pointers about why a stadium show should be as visually entertaining as it is musically."

Flying Solo

The tour started in Jacksonville, Florida, on May 23, 2001, and ended 11 months later in Orlando. Exhausted by the long and grueling tour, the five members of 'N Sync decided to take a few months off to relax and decide where their careers would take them next.

Recording a Solo Album

For his part, Justin did not intend to rest for long. He wanted to record a solo album, and after working with Traneau and the Neptunes, he wanted to explore R&B music further. Justin enjoyed the recordings of such R&B stars as Donny Hathaway, Marvin Gaye, Otis Redding, Stevie Wonder, Michael Jackson, Prince, and Al Green, and hoped to integrate some of their sounds into his music. He drafted Traneau and the Neptunes to help produce the album, and also called on the talents of R&B producer Tim Mosely, who is also known as Timbaland. Justin took a direct hand in the new record's production, and also cowrote all 13 songs.

The collaborative effort resulted in *Justified*, which was far different than anything 'N Sync had ever recorded. *Justified* was hardly kid stuff—songs like "Cry Me a River" showed that Justin had matured into an adult capable of singing with great emotion. Other tracks included the sexually charged "Rock Your Body," the hot Latin dance number "Señorita," and "Like I Love You," a soulful ballad performed with the accompaniment of **acoustic** instruments. Justin told *USA Today* that *Justified* was simply the next step in his development as a singer, saying:

> "This album makes perfect sense. It's not a departure from anything I've done, because I haven't done anything on my own. 'N Sync is great, but this is different—not only from 'N Sync, but from anything out there. I knew that when people first heard "Like I Love You," the consensus would be, 'What is this?' People aren't used to hearing me in this way, and it may take them a few listens to get it."

In May 2003, Justin went on tour to promote *Justified*. Unlike the prior 'N Sync tours, Justin's managers booked him into smaller concert halls. When Justin strode on stage, audiences saw a much different singer than they were used to seeing when he performed with 'N Sync. He trimmed off his dyed-blond curls and now wore a very-closely

JUSTIN TIMBERLAKE

Justin later admitted that his desire to embark on a solo career was a major reason that the members of 'N Sync decided to take a break from recording together. Justin worked with several well-known music producers because he wanted the music on his first album to be different from 'N Sync's sound.

trimmed buzz cut. The audience at the 22-year-old's shows was changing also. Where 'N Sync had mostly played to audiences of teens and pre-teens, Justin now appealed to fans in their 20s and 30s. He told *Rolling Stone*:

> "It's a liberating thing to walk out onstage and see people your age and up. And they're not screaming just because you're standing there, they're screaming because you did something to impress them. They don't put your poster on the wall—they just like your record."

Flying Solo 39

Surrounded by dancers, Justin performs a song on stage in London during his 2003 world tour. Justin's first single, "Like I Love You," reached number 11 on Billboard's chart. Two other singles from *Justified* did even better—"Cry Me a River" (number three) and "Rock Your Body" (number five)—and "Señorita" was another Top 40 hit.

The End of 'N Sync

It was clear that Justin intended to pursue a solo career. The other 'N Sync members had similar plans—Bass and Fatone had been offered acting jobs, Chasez had plans to cut his own solo album, and Kirkpatrick, now 32, knew he was well past the age in which he still held appeal to teen and pre-teen fans. In the past, successful boy bands like the New Kids on the Block had lasted about five years. 'N Sync had been together for seven years. While the band never officially broke up, all the members decided that it was probably time they moved on. Justin told *USA Today*:

> "I've been doing this since I was 12, and 'N Sync has been together for seven years. I honestly never expected things to get as big as they did.... It just got crazy, and I think we all knew we had to take a break, to figure things out."

Since recording *Celebrity*, the other four 'N Sync members have remained busy. Chasez has recorded two solo albums, titled *Schizophrenic* and *Kate*. Kirkpatrick started a new band, Little Red Monsters, and has done voice work for animated TV shows, including *The Fairly OddParents*. Fatone has appeared in Broadway musicals, including the hits *Little Shop of Horrors* and *Rent*, and in 2007 competed on the television reality series *Dancing with the Stars*. Bass has provided voices for animated shows, including *Kim Possible* and *Robot Chicken*. Bass and Fatone plan to star in a TV comedy series, *The Odd Couple*, which was originally a Broadway play and then a movie and hit television show during the 1970s.

Clearly, though, none of the other 'N Sync members have matched Justin's success. After *Justified* was released, Justin found himself in great demand. He appeared on *The Tonight Show* with Jay Leno and *Last Call* with Carson Daly, hosted *Saturday Night Live*, and sang "Like I Love You" during the MTV Video Music Awards. *Rolling Stone*, *Details*, *Teen People*, *Seventeen* and *Vibe* all wrote cover stories about Justin. *Rolling Stone* called Justin "The New King of Pop" and said, "He earned some cred, trading in teen beats for R&B swagger."

Hounded by the Tabloids

As Justin's fame spread, he found himself constantly followed by the tabloid press. After breaking up with Britney Spears, Justin was

Flying Solo 41

HOW BUSH FUMBLED THE 'WAR ON TERROR'

Rolling Stone

Issue 1009 >> September 21, 2006 >> $3.95

JUSTIN TIMBERLAKE

WET DREAM

THE NEW KING OF SEX GETS LOOSE

MICK, KEITH AND THE MAKING OF 'EXILE'
Wild Nights On the French Riviera

JOHN MAYER
Rock's Hot Soul Man

BEST FALL TV

Justin is featured on the cover of the September 2006 issue of *Rolling Stone* magazine. In 2003 the influential magazine referred to the young singer as "the New King of Pop," and commented that *Justified* showed that Justin had successfully made the transition from "boy band" singer to an artist with adult appeal.

JUSTIN TIMBERLAKE

photographed in the company of some of the entertainment world's most beautiful stars. He was first linked to Alyssa Milano, the star of the television series *Charmed*. Next, he was rumored to be in relationships with pop stars Janet Jackson and Christina Aguilera and film actress Jenna Dewan. However, most of the media attention centered on his relationship with movie star Cameron Diaz.

Through it all, Justin has tried to keep his personal life private. He has occasionally lashed out at the paparazzi, the celebrity-hunting photographers who seem to follow him wherever he goes.

In November 2004 Justin and Cameron were confronted by two photographers as they left the Château Marmont Hotel in Hollywood.

Cameron Diaz (left) and Justin began dating soon after meeting at the Kids' Choice Awards in April 2003. During the four years that the high-profile couple dated, they had several run-ins with the paparazzi. In one case, they grabbed a photographer's camera, later claiming that the photographer had ambushed them and that they were acting in self-defense.

Cameron reacted angrily, allegedly striking one of the men and knocking him to the ground. Justin is alleged to have also slapped the man while standing over him and threatening him further. A month after the incident, Justin was called before the district attorney, who told the singer to use better judgment the next time he is harassed by tabloid photographers. Since then, Justin has promised to behave better, but he makes no secret of his disdain for the paparazzi. He told *Rolling Stone*:

> "It's got to top the list of the world's creepiest professions. I've run the gamut with how I feel about it. I had the confrontation, where I slapped a paparazzo, and that was bad. I had to go meet the district attorney, who slapped the back of my hand and said I shouldn't retaliate with violence. . . . I love what I do, but I also love my life and my privacy."

Despite the incident in Hollywood, Justin did manage to share a lot of good times with Cameron. The two dated for about four years but by early 2007 that relationship had ended. The two stars remained tight-lipped about what led to the breakup. A joint statement released by their publicists read:

> "We have, in fact, ended our romantic relationship, and have done so mutually and as friends, with continued love and respect for one another."

That didn't stop the tabloid press from speculating about what led to the breakup. E! Online reported that Justin had started dating actress Scarlett Johansson behind Cameron's back, and had included her in a sexy music video. Reportedly, when Cameron saw the video she flew into a jealous rage. Meanwhile, the tabloids soon got hot on Justin's trail again, reporting that he was romantically involved with actresses Jessica Biel and Kate Hudson.

As for Justin, he remained steadfastly private—after his breakup with Cameron Diaz, he refused to admit to having a relationship with any specific woman. When *People* magazine asked him how he liked being single, he responded, "Right now, I want to enjoy life. I'm throwing it out there, seeing what happens. I'm testing the water, man."

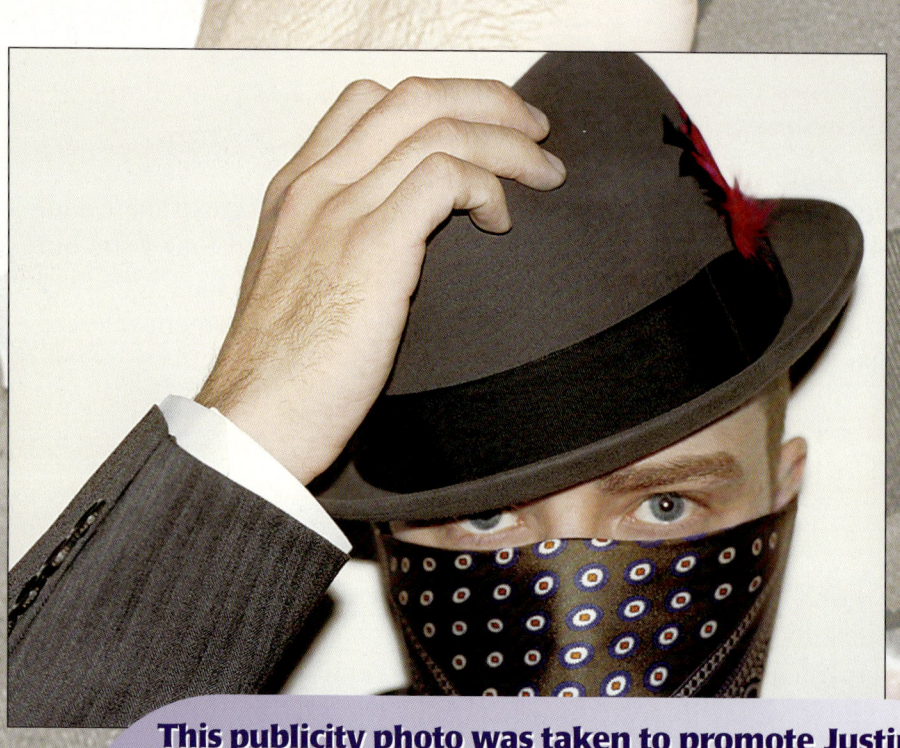

This publicity photo was taken to promote Justin's second solo album, *FutureSex/LoveSounds*, which was released in the fall of 2006. The album debuted in the top spot on Billboard's album chart and by the spring of 2007 had sold more than 6 million copies. Three singles from *FutureSex/LoveSounds* reached number one in the United States.

5

Limitless Options

Once *Justified* showed that Justin Timberlake could draw an audience on his own, it did not take long for Hollywood producers to come calling with offers to appear in films. Justin had always been interested in expanding his range as an entertainer and to act in nonmusical movie roles. Now he finally had the opportunity.

Justin was not exactly inexperienced: his role on the *All-New Mickey Mouse Club* had required some acting. As he forged a solo career, he had accepted **cameo** roles on several television shows, including *Sabrina the Teenage*

Witch, *Clueless*, *Mad TV*, and *Sesame Street*. In 2005 he showed a flair for comedy when he guest-hosted *Saturday Night Live*. The highlight of the show was a sketch he performed with comic Jimmy Fallon that spoofed the Bee Gees, the **disco** group from the 1970s. Justin played Robin Gibb, one of the three singing Gibb brothers who comprised the group. Fallon, who played Barry Gibb, told *Rolling Stone*:

> "He has great comic timing. We were all impressed. We were about to go live—and we had our backs to the audience—and Justin said to me, 'Remember the harmony on that one part. Seriously! Remember it.' I'll never forget that—I was nervous I wouldn't nail it."

High Marks for Acting

His performance on *Saturday Night Live* convinced producers he was ready to step into meatier roles. In 2005, he was cast for a supporting role in the film *Edison Force*, a crime drama starring Morgan Freeman and Kevin Spacey. Justin plays the role of Josh Pollack, a young **journalist**. However, the film turned out to be an abysmal failure. It was screened at the Toronto Film Festival, where it was panned by critics. Test audiences also turned thumbs down. The studio decided not to show the film in theaters, although in 2006 it was released in a DVD format.

By then, Justin was already involved in a much more highly regarded film project. He was cast in the role of Frankie Ballenbacher in the crime drama *Alpha Dog*. The film is based on a real case involving the kidnapping and murder of a 15-year-old boy by teenage thugs who wanted to collect a drug debt from the victim's older brother. Justin played one of the kidnappers. Other roles were played by Emile Hirsch, who portrayed the other kidnapper, Johnny Truelove, and Bruce Willis, who played Johnny's father.

Justin was given high marks for his acting in the film. *Chicago Sun-Times* film critic Miriam Di Nunzio wrote:

> "The movie's biggest surprise is Timberlake, who finds the heart and soul of the not-so-tough Frankie and makes him the film's most complete character. Timberlake is not the pretty-boy music maker here; Frankie is tattooed, foulmouthed and an all-around loser who would do anything to shine in Truelove's eyes."

Limitless Options

MORGAN FREEMAN   **LL COOL J**   **JUSTIN TIMBERLAKE** AND **KEVIN SPACEY**

EDISON

In the crime drama *Edison Force*, Justin starred with three experienced actors: LL Cool J, Kevin Spacey, and Morgan Freeman. In the film Justin's character is a journalist who helps to expose a corrupt police squad. However, test audiences did not respond well to the film and it was only released on DVD in the United States.

Other Film Projects

Following *Alpha Dog*, audiences saw Justin is another dramatic role when he played Ronnie, the boyfriend of the character portrayed by Christina Ricci in the quirky film *Black Snake Moan*. The 2007 movie is about an aging blues musician, played by Samuel L. Jackson, who helps straighten out the life of Ricci's character, Rae, by chaining her to his radiator. Justin told *Entertainment Weekly*:

48 JUSTIN TIMBERLAKE

In the 2006 film *Alpha Dog* Justin starred as Frankie, a tattooed wannabe gangster from the suburbs who helps a drug dealer friend kidnap a 15-year-old boy. The movie, which was based on a true story, was a modest hit, earning more than $20 million in theaters before being released on DVD in the spring of 2007.

Limitless Options

> "I love the movie. I want to be involved in things that are inspiring to me. I guess I just have to trust my taste barometer."

Following *Black Snake Moan*, Justin provided the voice for the character of Artie—a young King Arthur—in the animated film *Shrek the Third*, the third installment of the enormously popular series about the adventures of a grumpy green ogre. He will also be featured in *Southland Tales*, a futuristic thriller about a terrorist attack on the U.S. Justin plays a disfigured veteran of the Iraq War who also serves as

Director Craig Brewer offers suggestions to Justin on the set of *Black Snake Moan*. Several movie critics singled out Justin's acting for praise. "His serious acting performances in a recent pair of indie-fest films—*Alpha Dog* and *Black Snake Moan*—have scored a collective thumbs-up," wrote Brian McCollum in the *Detroit Free Press*.

narrator of the film. Justin told *Rolling Stone* that his work in film enables him to display a different side of his talent, saying:

> "The reason I got into film is because I needed something inspiring, but more intimate, that I didn't have to do in front of 18,000 people every night."

A Second Solo Album

Perhaps it was due to the heavy schedule of making films, cutting records, and touring, but in 2006 Justin acknowledged that at times he has used the illegal drug marijuana. He told *Rolling Stone* that he smoked pot heavily during the recording sessions for *Justified*, and has since then acknowledged smoking marijuana from time to time. However, he also said that he would not use drugs when working on future movie or music projects, such as his second solo album, *FutureSex/LoveSounds*.

As the title suggests, the album is chock-full of songs meant to bring lovers together—particularly the title track, "FutureSex." The song features the lyric, "I'm bringing sexy back." To produce the album, he called again on the talents of Timbaland. Together, they decided to delve further into the R&B sound that had dominated *Justified*. This time Justin sought to emulate the sounds of Prince, one of the major artists working in R&B during the 1980s and 1990s. He told the Allentown *Morning Call*:

> "Prince to me is the ultimate artist. It's like the biggest understatement to say that someone like Prince influences someone like me, who grew up listening to all his work. The thing that I love about Prince is he really makes his own rules and I think that creating something like music, you really shouldn't have any rules."

There is no question that *FutureSex/LoveSounds* represents another effort by Justin to put distance between himself and the boy band sound of 'N Sync. To promote the album, Justin embarked on a nationwide tour. The venues on the tour included nightclubs, concert halls, and theaters, some of which were closed to fans under the age of 18. Even though the album is not geared to young fans, it has still sold very well. By early 2007, *FutureSex/LoveSounds* had sold more than 6 million

Limitless Options   51

JUSTIN TIMBERLAKE
FUTURESEX/LOVESOUNDS

FutureSex/LoveSounds received good reviews in many publications when it was released in September 2006. "It's hard not to be swayed by the persuasive minimalist funk and hip-hop grooves that [Justin] and a team of producers (including Timbaland and Rick Rubin) have concocted," wrote music critic Cary Darling in the *Fort Worth Star-Telegram*.

copies. Critics suggested the album featured Timberlake's best work. Said *People* magazine music critic Chuck Arnold:

> "Working again with 'Cry Me a River' producer Timbaland—who's probably got the best beats in the business right now—Timberlake delivers highlight after highlight."

JUSTIN TIMBERLAKE

What the Future Holds

While some boy bands, such as the Backstreet Boys, have gotten back together for reunion shows, Justin doesn't see that happening with 'N Sync. He told the *Morning Call*:

> **"I think what we did doesn't work anymore. I think it's kind of hard to make something work that was kind of a moment in time, especially when you're all such different people now."**

Justin's music may not be intended for young fans, but he had not forgotten them, either. Justin hopes that he can serve as an inspiration to young singers and musicians to pursue careers in music. In 2001, he

Since becoming a celebrity, Justin has generously given his time and money to several charitable causes. Here the singer poses with workers in a McDonald's restaurant in Milan, Italy, while taking part in World Children's Day, a global fundraiser to benefit Ronald McDonald House Charities and local children's causes in more than 100 countries.

established the Justin Timberlake Foundation to support music and art education in public schools. He pointed out that when he was a young boy growing up in Millington, most of his music education was provided by a private teacher, Bob Westbrook, and not by his elementary school. Justin said he was inspired to start the foundation after the 1999 massacre of students at Columbine High School in Colorado, when two students smuggled guns into the school and went on a shooting rampage before taking their own lives. Justin has wondered whether the killers would have resorted to bloodshed if they had an alternative path, such as music, in which they could have worked through their hostilities. He told *Rolling Stone*:

> "I grew up in the boondocks, and there just wasn't a good musical program at school. I've thought about it a little bit—this and the whole Columbine incident. Music is another way for young minds and young bodies to express themselves, to find a way to get all those negative thoughts and energies out."

In 2002, the Justin Timberlake Foundation partnered with the Carlsbad, California-based American Music Conference to help raise awareness of the importance of music education in elementary schools. He has used his appearances on television interview shows to promote the association and urge viewers to donate to the group. Justin has also headed an effort to gather names on petitions urging lawmakers to increase funding for school music programs. In 2002 Justin's mother Lynn Harless delivered petitions to members of Congress calling on more support for music education in U.S. schools.

In addition to singing, acting and his work for his foundation, Justin is also looking into other ventures. In 2006, he launched a clothing line with a friend, Trace Ayala, whom he has known since childhood. Their company, William Rast, produces blue jeans, sweatshirts, hoodies, T-shirts, and other sportswear. (The company draws its name from Justin's grandfather's first name, William, and Ayala's grandfather's last name, Rast.) Justin took a hands-on approach to designing the styles and believes the clothes reflect a young, hip look. He told *USA Today* that he has remained behind the scenes because he feels its product is so strong that the company does not need him to help boost sales:

54 JUSTIN TIMBERLAKE

Justin is slimed while hosting the 2007 Kids' Choice Awards ceremony in New York. Many people believe that Justin will only become more popular. "This kid's going to be the biggest star that ever hit anywhere," commented *Alpha Dog* director Nick Cassavetes, while Jive Records president Barry Weiss says, "He is hugely important to the [music] industry."

Limitless Options

> **"We want the brand to exist on its own. That's why you haven't seen me doing any kind of print [advertising] campaign."**

As Timberlake looks forward to the rest of his career, he knows there will be movie offers on the table as well as opportunities to record new albums. At this point, he is not sure how much longer his music career will continue. He has talked about quitting when he reaches the age of 30 in 2011, and then finding a new creative interest to pursue. He told *Rolling Stone*, "The dream is to be able to have a schedule like I've had in the last five years, to put out a record and tour, then take a little break, maybe do some films." He added, "Just float around—not too shabby, right?"

CHRONOLOGY

1981 Justin Randall Timberlake born January 31 in Millington, Tennessee.

1990 First performs for an audience during an elementary school talent show.

1992 Wins first major talent contest, the Universal Charm Pageant.

1993 Wins a role on the *All-New Mickey Mouse Club*.

1995 Disney cancels the *All-New Mickey Mouse Club*; Justin joins 'N Sync.

1996 'N Sync releases its first album, *'N Sync*, in Europe; the band tours the European continent and other countries.

1998 *'N Sync* released in the United States; Justin starts dating Britney Spears.

1999 'N Sync breaks with manager Lou Pearlman and signs with Jive Records.

2000 'N Sync releases *No Strings Attached*; readers of *People* vote Justin "The Most Beautiful Person in the World."

2001 'N Sync releases *Celebrity*.

2002 Justin and Britney break up.

2003 Justin's first solo album, *Justified*, is released; other 'N Sync members pursue their own solo careers.

2004 During a halftime performance at the Super Bowl, Justin pulls down Janet Jackson's top in what he later described as a "wardrobe malfunction." A week later, he apologizes on national TV while picking up two Grammy Awards for *Justified*. Also starts dating Cameron Diaz.

2005 Spoofs the Bee Gees in a *Saturday Night Live* sketch; plays a supporting role in his first film, *Edison Force*.

2006 Acknowledges marijuana use in a *Rolling Stone* interview; releases *FutureSex/LoveSounds*; plays roles in the films *Alpha Dog* and *Black Snake Moan*.

2007 Wins two more Grammy Awards; lends his voice to the animated film *Shrek the Third*.

ACCOMPLISHMENTS & AWARDS

Albums
With 'N Sync
1998 *'N Sync; Home for Christmas*
2000 *No Strings Attached*
2001 *Celebrity*

Solo
2002 *Justified*
2006 *FutureSex/LoveSounds*

Television
1993–1995 *The All-New Mickey Mouse Club*

Films
2006 *Edison Force*
2007 *Alpha Dog*; *Black Snake Moan*; *Shrek the Third*; *Southland Tales* (planned release)

Awards and Recognition
With 'N Sync
1998 Winner, *Billboard* Video Music Awards for Best Dance and Best New Artist for "I Want You Back"

1999 Winner, American Music Award for Favorite Pop/Rock New Artist

Winner, Blockbuster Award for Favorite New Artist-Group

Winner, Teen Choice Award for Album of the Year for *'N Sync*

2000 Nominated for Grammy Awards for Best Pop Collaboration with Vocals for "Music Of My Heart" with Gloria Estefan and Best Country Collaboration with Vocals for "God Must Have Spent A Little More Time On You" with Alabama

Winner, Blockbuster Award for Favorite Song from a Movie for "Music Of My Heart"

Winner, Teen Choice Awards for Choice Single, Choice Music Video, and Song of the Summer for "Bye Bye Bye" and Choice Pop Group

Winner, MTV Video Music Awards for Viewer's Choice, Best Pop Video, and Best Choreography for "Bye Bye Bye"

Winner, Much Music Video Award for People's Choice-Favorite International Group

"Bye Bye Bye" named 55th on the list of 100 Greatest Pop Songs by *Rolling Stone* and MTV

ACCOMPLISHMENTS & AWARDS

Winner, Radio Music Awards for Song of the Year: Top 40/Pop Radio (for "Bye Bye Bye") and Artist of the Year: Top 40/Pop Radio

2001 Winner, American Music Award for Internet Fans Artist of the Year Award

Winner, People's Choice Award for Favorite Musical Group or Band

Nominated for Grammy Awards for Record of the Year and Best Pop Vocal Performance by a Duo or Group for "Bye Bye Bye" and Best Pop Vocal Album for *No Strings Attached*

Winner, Blockbuster Entertainment Awards for Favorite CD, Favorite Group-Pop, and Favorite Single for "Bye Bye Bye"

Winner, Teen Choice Awards for Choice Single for "Pop," Choice Album for *Celebrity*, and Choice Concert

Winner, MTV Video Music Awards for Best Group Video, Best Pop Video, Best Dance Video, and Viewer's Choice for "Pop"

2002 Winner, People's Choice Award for Favorite Musical Group or Band

Winner, American Music Award for Favorite Pop/Rock Band/Duo/Group

Nominated for Grammy Awards for Best Pop Performance by a Duo or Group with Vocal for "Gone" and Best Pop Vocal Album for *Celebrity*

Winner, Teen Choice Awards for Choice Single and Choice Hook Up for "Girlfriend" with Nelly

Nominated for a Grammy Award for Best Pop Performance by a Duo or Group with Vocal for "Girlfriend"

Solo

2000 Winner, Teen Choice Awards for Male Hottie of the Year

2001 Winner, Teen Choice Awards for Male Hottie of the Year

2002 Nominated for Grammy Award for Best Pop Collaboration with Brian McKnight for "My Kind of Girl"

2003 Nominated for Grammy Award for Best Rap/Sung Collaboration with Clipse for "Like I Love You"

Winner, MTV Video Music Awards for Best Pop Video and Best Male Video for "Cry Me a River" and Best Dance Video for "Rock Your Body"

ACCOMPLISHMENTS & AWARDS

Winner, World Music Award for Best-Selling Dance Artist

Winner, Radio Music Award for Artist of the Year-Top 40 Radio

Winner, MTV Europe Awards for Best Male Artist, Best Album, and Best Pop Award for *Justified*

Winner, American Music Award for Favorite Pop/Rock Album for *Justified*

Winner of *Rolling Stone* readers' poll as Best Album of the Year for *Justified*, Artist of the Year, Best Male Performer, and Best Tour, and in *Rolling Stone* critics' poll as Best Male Performer

2004 Nominated for Grammy Award for Album of the Year for *Justified*

Nominated for Grammy Award for Record of the Year for "Where is the Love" with the Black Eyed Peas

Winner of Grammy Award for Best Pop Vocal Album for *Justified*

Winner of Grammy Award for Best Male Pop Vocal Performance for "Cry Me a River"

Winner, Brit Awards for Best International Album for *Justified* and Best International Male Artist

2006 Winner, MTV Music Awards for Best Male Artist and Best Pop Artist

2007 Nominated for Grammy Award for Album of the Year for *FutureSex/LoveSounds*

Nominated for Grammy Award for Best Pop Vocal Album for *FutureSex/LoveSounds*

Winner of Grammy Award for Best Rap/Sung Collaboration for "My Love" with T.I.

Winner of Grammy Award for Best Dance Recording for "SexyBack"

Winner, Brit Award for Best International Male Solo Artist

FURTHER READING & INTERNET RESOURCES

Books

Grabowsky, John F. *'N Sync*. Philadelphia: Chelsea House, 2000.

Smith, Sean. *Justin: The Unauthorized Biography*. New York: Pocket Books, 2004.

Squires, K.M. *'N Sync: The Official Book*. New York: Bantam Doubleday Dell Books for Young Readers, 1998.

Periodicals

Arnold, Chuck. "Justin Timberlake, *FutureSex/LoveSounds*," *People*, vol. 66, no. 12 (September 18, 2006): p. 47.

Collis, Clark, and Neil Drumming, "Sexy Beast," *Entertainment Weekly*, no. 920 (February 9, 2007): p. 32.

Eliscu, Jenny. "The New King of Pop," *Rolling Stone*, nos. 938-939 (December 25, 2003–January 8, 2004): p. 44.

Moser, John J. "He Justifies Some Fresh Prince: In Sync with Timbaland, Justin Timberlake Moves to Club R&B," *Allentown Morning Call* (September 16, 2006).

Scaggs, Austin. "Justin Timberlake Revs Up His Sex Machine," *Rolling Stone*, no. 1,009 (Sept. 21, 2006): p. 50.

Web Sites

www.justintimberlake.com
Fans who visit Justin Timberlake's official Web site will find a schedule of the singer's tour dates, photos of Justin, some of his videos, and a discography of his music.

www.nsync.com
Fans of the boy band can continue to receive updates on the members through 'N Sync's official Web site. The site includes biographies of the singers, latest developments in their careers, photos and tour dates and other appearances by the singers as they pursue their solo projects.

www.amc-music.com/partners/timberlake.htm
Web site maintained by the American Music Conference, which has partnered with the Justin Timberlake Foundation to support music education in public schools. Visitors to the site can follow the activities of the conference, such as its support for Drum Month, which includes programs each November to encourage young people to learn about percussion instruments, and Music In Our Schools Month, an annual event each March in which members contact political leaders and ask for support for music education.

GLOSSARY

acoustic—musical instruments, particularly guitars, that do not rely on electronic amplification to produce sound.

audition—a test—usually a short performance—given by a person who is applying for a role on a television show, movie, or play.

cameo—a brief (and often unannounced and uncredited) appearance by a celebrity on a television show or in a film.

choreographers—professionals who design and direct dance performances.

disco—a style of dance music popular during the 1970s that featured fast-paced and heavy, pulsating electronically produced beats.

journalist—a professional who gathers and writes the news for the print, electronic, and on-line media.

lawsuit—a legal action started by a person who believes he has been wronged by another; typically, the party that files the lawsuit seeks monetary compensation.

lip synch—to pretend to sing a song by moving the lips but without actually uttering the words, which are provided through a recording played for an audience.

marionettes—puppets, typically fashioned from wood, that are manipulated by strings attached to their hands, feet, and head and controlled from above the stage by the puppeteer.

narrator—a character in a book, play or film who speaks directly to the audience, usually to explain the story.

pyrotechnics—in entertainment, the use of fireworks, smoke, lasers, spotlights, and other techniques to add visual excitement to the show.

sketch comedy—style of comedy produced through acting out a very short play on stage or television.

studio—a place established for an artist to work, usually featuring the tools and equipment necessary to perform the art, such as recording music.

tabloid—a style of journalism that concentrates on sensational crime, scandals, and gossip about celebrities; the name stems from the format of the newspapers (known as tabloids) that originally specialized in that style of news.

tutors—private teachers hired to educate one student or a small group of students.

venues—stadiums, arenas, concert halls, auditoriums, and similar places where entertainers would be booked to perform.

INDEX

Aguilera, Christina, 11, 18, 19, 42
The All-New Mickey Mouse Club, 8, 16, 18–19, 20, 28, 45
Alpha Dog (film), 46–47, 48, 49, 54
Arnold, Chuck, 51
Ayala, Trace, 53

Bass, Lance, 20, 21, 40
Biel, Jessica, 43
Black Snake Moan (film), 47, 49
Bomar, Bill (grandfather), 14
Brewer, Craig, 49
"Bye Bye Bye" (single), 31

Cassavetes, Nick, 54
Celebrity (album), 34, 36–37, 40
charity work, 52–53
Chasez, J.C., 20, 21, 23, 25–26, 40
childhood, 13–14, 16
"Cry Me a River" (single), 6, 8, 9–11, 37, 39

Daly, Carson, 40
Darling, Cary, 51
dating. *See* romantic relationships
Dewan, Jenna, 42
Di Nunzio, Miriam, 46
Diaz, Cameron, 42–43

Edison Force (film), 46, 47

Fallon, Jimmy, 46
Fatone, Joey, 20, 21, 40
Fischetti, Bob, 26
Freeman, Morgan, 46, 47
FutureSex/LoveSounds (album), 44–45, 50–51

Grammy Awards, 6–7, 8, 11

Harless, Lynn (mother), 12, 14, 16, 21, 53
Harless, Paul (stepfather), 14, 16, 21
Hedegaard, Erik, 10–11
Hirsch, Emile, 46
Home for Christmas (album), 28
Hudson, Kate, 43
Hugo, Chad, 34

"I Want You Back" (single), 21

Jackson, Janet, 7–8, 9, 26, 42
Jackson, Samuel L., 47
Jive Records, 31, 33
Johansson, Scarlett, 43
Justified (album), 6, 8, 10–11, 37–39, 41, 45, 50
Justin Timberlake Foundation, 52–53

Kate (album), 40
Kids' Choice Awards, 42, 54
Kirkpatrick, Chris, 18, 20–21, 40

Leno, Jay, 26, 40
"Like I Love You" (single), 8, 39
Little Red Monsters, 40
LL Cool J, 46, 47

marijuana, 50
Martin, Max, 21
McCollum, Brian, 49
Milano, Alyssa, 42
Mosely, Tim (Timbaland), 37
MTV Video Music Awards, 40

'N Sync, 8, 25–27, 34, 36–37, 40, 52
  awards won by, 24
  is formed, 20–23
  with Jive Records, 31–33
  lawsuit of, against Pearlman, 28–31

INDEX

'N Sync (album), 21–23, 26
No Strings Attached (album), 31–33, 34

Pearlman, Lou, 20–23, 26, 34
   lawsuit of, against 'N Sync, 28–31
People magazine, 33, 34
"Pop" (single), 34, 36
Presley, Elvis, 14, 15
Prince, 50

Ricci, Christina, 47
Rodman, Sarah, 36
romantic relationships, 8–11, 28–29, 42–43
Rubin, Rick, 51

Saturday Night Live, 11, 46
Schenkenberg, Marcus, 8
Schizophrenic (album), 40
Shrek the Third (film), 49
Smith, Sean (Justin), 14, 21, 25–26, 34
Southland Tales (film), 49–50
Spacey, Kevin, 46, 47
Spears, Britney, 8–11, 18, 19, 28–29, 40
Squires, K.M. ('N Sync: The Official Book), 18
Star Search, 16–17, 18
Super Bowl (2004), 7–8, 9, 11

Teen Choice Awards, 24
Timbaland (Tim Mosely), 37, 50
Timberlake, Justin
   and the 2004 Super Bowl, 7–8, 9, 11
   acting career, 45–50, 55
   on The All-New Mickey Mouse Club, 8, 16, 18–19, 20, 45
   awards won by, 6–7, 11, 24
   birth and childhood, 13–14, 16
   business ventures, 53, 55
   charity work, 52–53
   critical reception of, 10, 36, 46, 49, 51
   and golf, 33–34, 35
   and marijuana, 50
   in 'N Sync, 8, 20–33, 34, 36–37, 40
   as "The New King of Pop," 40–41
   and the paparazzi, 42–43
   as People's "Most Beautiful Person," 33
   romantic relationships, 8–11, 28–29, 42–43
   on Saturday Night Live, 11, 46
   solo career, 37–41, 44–45, 50–51
   songwriting, 31, 34, 37
   wins the Universal Charm Pageant, 16
Timberlake, Randall (father), 14
Traneau, Brian, 34, 37
Truelove, Johnny, 46

Universal Charm Pageant, 16

Volle, Dag, 21

Weiss, Barry, 8, 54
Westbrook, Bob, 12, 14, 16, 21, 53
William Rast (clothing company), 53, 55
Williams, Pharrell, 34
Willis, Bruce, 46
World Children's Day, 52

Yerger, Chuck, 25–26

ABOUT THE AUTHOR

Hal Marcovitz lives in Chalfont, Pennsylvania, with his wife Gail and daughters Ashley and Michelle. He is the author of nearly 100 books for young readers, including *LeBron James* and *Lindsay Lohan* in the Mason Crest series POP CULTURE: A VIEW FROM THE PAPARAZZI.

Picture Credits

page

- **2:** AdMedia/Sipa Press
- **6:** Abaca Press/MCT
- **9:** WENN Photos
- **10:** Hector Mata/AFP
- **12:** Kevin Mazur/WireImage
- **15:** MGM/NMI
- **17:** Star Max Photos
- **19:** Walt Disney Studio/NMI
- **20:** Jive Records/FPS
- **22:** UPI Photo Archive
- **24:** UPI Photo Archive
- **27:** Star Max Photos
- **29:** Star Max Photos
- **30:** Newswire Photo Archive
- **32:** Reuters Photo Archive
- **35:** Newswire Photo Archive
- **36:** Reuters Photo Archive
- **38:** Jive/Zomba/KRT
- **39:** Reuters Photo Archive
- **41:** New Millennium Images
- **42:** London Entertainment/Splash
- **44:** Jive Records/Newswire Photos
- **47:** Nu Image Films/NMI
- **48:** Universal Pictures/NMI
- **49:** Paramount Classic/NMI
- **51:** Jive Records/Newswire Photos
- **52:** Newswire Photo Archive
- **54:** NewsFoto/Nickelodeon

Front cover: NewsFoto Service/Nickelodeon
Back cover: ZUMA Press